Magical Friendship Stories

ORCHARD BOOKS

First published in 2017 in Poland by Egmont Poland
First published in Great Britain in 2018 by The Watts Publishing Group

1 3 5 7 9 10 8 6 4 2

A CIP catalogue record for this book is available from the British Library.

HB ISBN 978 1 40835 620 3
PB ISBN 978 1 40835 793 4

Printed and bound in China

Orchard Books
An imprint of Hachette Children's Group
Part of The Watts Publishing Group Limited
Carmelite House
50 Victoria Embankment
London EC4Y 0DZ

An Hachette UK Company
www.hachette.co.uk

www.hachettechildrens.co.uk

Prologue

Twilight Sparkle, Rarity, Fluttershy, Applejack, Rainbow Dash, Pinkie Pie and Spike are the best of friends. Working together to maintain the peace and tranquility of Equestria, their beloved home, they discover an important message – that true friends are always there when you need them!

Canterlot Boutique

Rarity had just received some very good news. For a long time Rarity had dreamed of opening a boutique in Canterlot and finally the perfect location was available!

Rarity travelled to the city at once and worked very hard to make her shop the most beautiful in all of Canterlot.

When Rarity invited her friends to see the shop, they were amazed. “Do you like it?” she asked.

“It’s lovely,” Fluttershy smiled.

“Gosh, Rarity. I know hard work when I see it, and it looks like you worked your hooves to the nub!” said Applejack.

Rarity was so proud of her new shop.

“The boutique would never have been ready for its grand opening without the help of my new manager, Sassy Saddles,” Rarity admitted.

Sassy Saddles had worked in all of the finest boutiques in Canterlot so Rarity was thrilled to have her as the manager for the Canterlot Boutique. Sassy shared her ideas to make the shop a huge success.

Sassy made sure that everything in Rarity's collection was exactly what the fashionable fillies in Canterlot wanted. "It turns out that everypony here loves royalty!" Sassy revealed.

"So I created a brand new collection that reflects the royalty of Canterlot," Rarity explained.

"And even better," Rarity said. " You are the most popular princess in Canterlot, Twilight Sparkle! So my most fabulous gown is inspired by your coronation."

Rarity revealed her newest collection to her friends. She explained how each new dress was based on her new rules, 'Rarity's Rules of TLC'.

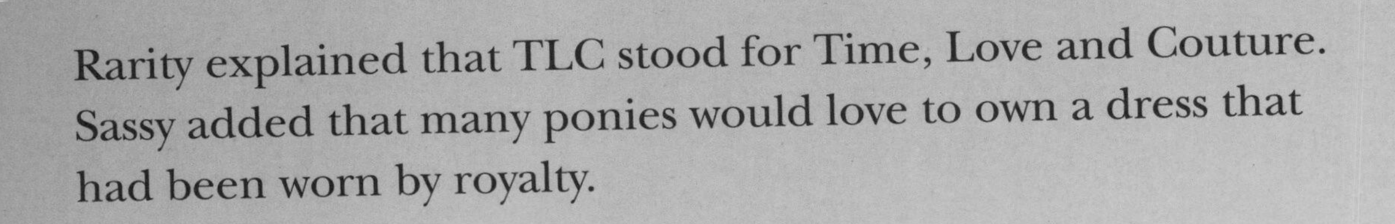

Rarity explained that TLC stood for Time, Love and Couture. Sassy added that many ponies would love to own a dress that had been worn by royalty.

"So, Twilight, we were wondering if you might possibly wear this special dress tonight?" Rarity asked, shyly.

Twilight was more than happy to help.

Finally it was time for Canterlot Boutique to open. "Ever since I was a little filly, all I've ever wanted was to own a boutique here in Canterlot," Rarity admitted, giddy with excitement.

Rarity couldn't wait to welcome the Canterlot ponies outside. She opened the door, took a deep breath and ...

"Welcome to the grand opening of Canterlot Boutique!" said Sassy Saddles.

Rarity was upset that she hadn't been first to welcome the ponies.

"That Sassy totally stepped on your hooves, Rarity," said Applejack.

But Rarity was sure Sassy didn't do it on purpose. She trusted her manager completely.

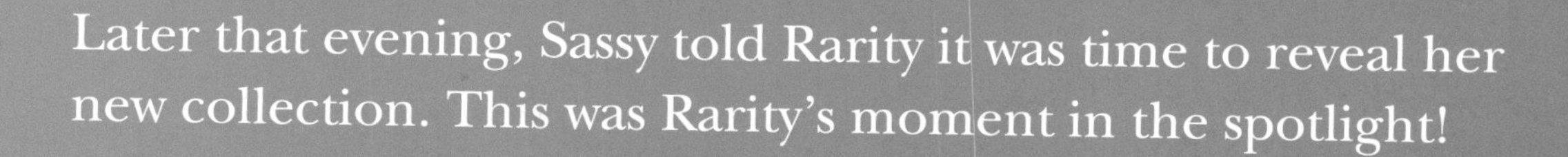

Later that evening, Sassy told Rarity it was time to reveal her new collection. This was Rarity's moment in the spotlight!

"Fillies and gentlecolts! My name is Rarity and I'd like to welcome you – again – to the grand opening of Canterlot Boutique," she said, looking at the crowd confidently. "I'm thrilled that you are here to see my newest collection inspired by this regal city!"

Rarity drew the curtains and revealed her latest collection.

“My favourite part of being a designer is finding inspiration,” she explained to the crowd. “These two whimsical creations are based on Princesses Celestia and Luna, and their bond with the Sun and Moon.”

Rarity’s Royal Regalia collection was an instant success. And once everypony saw Twilight Sparkle in the Princess Dress, everypony in Canterlot wanted one!

Sassy Saddles started taking orders for the gown while Rarity’s friends congratulated her on the new collection.

After the grand opening, Rarity was shocked to see Sassy had taken one hundred orders for the Princess Dress! She didn't want to disappoint her customers so she got to work.

But as she made each dress, the pile of orders got higher and higher. After a while, Rarity had made so many identical dresses that they were no longer unique.

Just as Rarity finished the first set of orders, Sassy brought in another hundred! But Rarity had had enough.

"If this is what success looks like, I want no part of it!" Rarity said angrily. "Make up flyers for a closing down sale! I'm closing Canterlot Boutique!"

Sassy was distraught but Rarity wouldn't budge.

But Sassy had an idea. During the sale she only showed ponies the other gowns from the Royal Regalia collection.

The Canterlot ponies loved all the different dresses and everypony found one perfect for them. Rarity remembered why she loved being a designer – she could make other ponies happy! So Rarity decided not to close Canterlot Boutique after all.

And Rarity was happy to have Sassy stay as the manager so they could work to make the boutique a success, together.

the end

The Mane Attraction

The ponies were organising the annual Helping Hooves Festival and Applejack was overseeing the organisation. Pinkie Pie had managed to book the most famous pop singer in Equestria – Countess Coloratura. She was so excited!

Applejack said she already knew somepony called Coloratura, but she definitely wasn't a countess. Pinkie Pie asked Applejack what her cutie mark was and Applejack remembered it was colourful music notes.

Pinkie Pie was speechless – maybe they were talking about the same pony!

Applejack told everypony how she and Rara – that was what she called Coloratura – had had the best time at Camp Friendship. The two ponies had performed together at the camp talent show! Applejack said she and Rara were great friends.

Applejack couldn't believe Rara had become a famous singer! When Coloratura arrived at the Festival, Applejack asked if she remembered her. She did!

But before they could talk properly, Coloratura's manager, Svengallop, interrupted them and led her away.

"Where is the pony Pinkie Pie?" asked Svengallop.

"I'm the pony Pinkie Pie, Mr. Manager, sir!" Pinkie Pie replied quickly.

"Do you have the water imported from Rainbow Falls that I requested for Countess Coloratura?" Svengallop demanded.

"Of course!" said Pinkie Pie. She had prepared everything for the concert. Satisfied, Svengallop decided it was time for rehearsal.

Everypony was impressed with the performance except Applejack. This wasn't the cute and spontaneous pony she had made friends with at camp.

But Svengallop was delighted with Coloratura. "Oh, my shining star! Thanks to the sparkling costume, dazzling choreography and brilliant song I wrote, your performance was spectacular!" he exclaimed.

Applejack began to be very suspicious of Svengallop.

"Correct me if I'm wrong, but that fella isn't complimenting Rara. He's complimenting all the bells and whistles he's piled on to make her Countess Coloratura," said Applejack.

"Creating a performance is a lot of work. Countess Coloratura wouldn't be the same without all the extras," said Rarity.

But Applejack wasn't convinced. "If you ask me, that wouldn't be a bad thing," she replied.

Meanwhile, it was time for Countess Coloratura to meet the schoolponies.

Svengallop thought it was a waste of time but the singer told him it was her favourite part of any event. Applejack was very happy to hear this.

"As part of the Helping Hooves Festival, I'm holding a competition to give you a chance to sing with me onstage!" said Coloratura with a smile.

Everypony cheered and Applejack finally recognised her old friend. But then she overheard Svengallop shouting at Pinkie Pie.

Svengallop wanted Appleloosan oats and five hundred pre-peeled, pre-cored apples in the next twenty-four hours. "But that's impossible!" gasped Pinkie Pie.

"Do you want Countess Coloratura to perform tomorrow?" threatened Svengallop.

Applejack offered to talk to Coloratura and set things straight. But when Applejack spoke to Coloratura, she didn't receive the reply she thought she would.

"Svengallop works very hard as my manager," she said. "So if he needs something, I don't see anything wrong with that."

"Well do you see somethin' wrong with him tellin' Pinkie if she doesn't get those things he'll pull you from our charity festival?" Applejack retorted in frustration.

Countess Coloratura didn't believe Applejack. She thought her friend was just jealous of her success.

So Applejack said she would get proof and asked Coloratura to go along with her plan to find out Svengallop's true intentions.

Coloratura told Svengallop she wanted to cancel the contest with the schoolponies. Svengallop was thrilled! He ordered Pinkie Pie to make all the necessary changes in the schedule.

"Make the changes or Coloratura won't perform at your festival!" he threatened. But he didn't realise the conversation was being recorded by Twilight.

When Svengallop went to tell Coloratura, Twilight played his conversation with Pinkie Pie on the big screen. Coloratura was furious but Svengallop was too proud to admit his mistake so he left.

Coloratura was nervous about performing without Svengallop there.

"The best thing about friendship is gettin' to see your friend bein' true to their self," Applejack explained. "And Rara, when you're yourself, you're the brightest star I've ever seen."

When it was time to perform, Coloratura announced that she was simply Rara now and she sang a song of her own.

Everypony cheered when she finished singing – they loved Coloratura's new song!

To say thanks to her true friends, Coloratura invited Applejack and the Cutie Mark Crusaders on stage to sing with her. She had never been so happy!

the end

Viva Las Pegasus

Fluttershy and Applejack were in a state of shock, the Cutie Map was sending them to ... Las Pegasus!

"All those lights and sounds, not to mention the crowds ... Oh, just the thought of it is overwhelming!" Fluttershy cried.

Twilight Sparkle knew the ponies wouldn't enjoy the city, but she was sure that if they were called there by the map, their talents would definitely be needed to solve the friendship problem.

When they arrived, the ponies thought Las Pegasus was even worse than they imagined! But Fluttershy and Applejack wouldn't give up. The first pony they met was Gladmane, the resort manager.

"I'm what you might call a friendship connoisseur, so naturally I'm familiar with the friends of the great Twilight Sparkle! Applejack, Fluttershy, it's an honour to have you here." Gladmane offered to take them on a tour.

Gladmane introduced them to the director of the resort's show who invited them backstage. Fluttershy gasped with excitement when she saw some pink prairie dogs! Gladmane said he thought of all his employees as friends and everypony seemed to like him.

"Doesn't look like there's any friendship problem here," Applejack said quietly.

"There doesn't seem to be anything wrong around here at all," Fluttershy agreed. She had barely finished speaking when she heard a familiar voice.

"Ladies and gentleponies, I know you've come to this fair city to be entertained and I assure you there is nothing more entertaining than the astounding acrobatics act in Gladmane's show," said one of the voices.

"That might be true, if it weren't for the far superior, show-stopping exotic animal act!" another familiar voice replied.

Applejack and Fluttershy couldn't believe what they were hearing. Surely it couldn't be who they thought?

But Applejack recognised them at once – they were the voices of Flim and Flam! And it appeared that the two brothers were not getting along at all.

"You don't suppose we've been brought here to help them?" Fluttershy wondered.

"Absolutely not!" replied Applejack, appalled.

Gladmane admitted that he was worried about the two ponies. He said they had been arguing ever since they got to Las Pegasus. He gave them jobs to try to help but it only made everything worse.

But Applejack was sure that there had to be another problem in Las Pegasus.

"You don't pull a rabbit out of a hat on a trapeze!" Applejack overheard the director shouting.

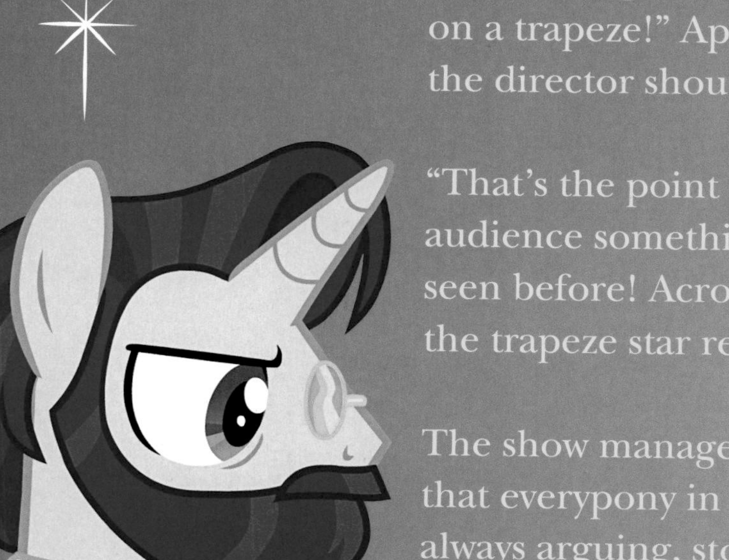

"That's the point – to give the audience something they've never seen before! Acrobatic magic!" the trapeze star replied.

The show manager told Applejack that everypony in the show was always arguing, stopping the team from realising their true potential.

That was perfect – the friendship problem Applejack was looking for! She was about to tell Fluttershy when she overheard another argument.

"I thought you two were friends," Applejack said.

"We were but we just can't seem to agree on anything anymore. We used to perform all over Equestria, but if we can't agree on a new act, we might as well stay at Gladmane's forever," one of the ponies replied.

Applejack was excited that there were two friendship problems to solve! And Fluttershy reminded her about another problem, Flim and Flam.

Suddenly Fluttershy realised that Gladmane would benefit from every broken friendship. He was making ponies fight on purpose!

"There must be a way to trick him into telling the truth!" Applejack said.

Fluttershy suggested a pair of ponies who were capable of tricking a trickster – Flim and Flam! The only catch was that Applejack would have to help them with their friendship problem.

"Do either of you even know what you're fightin' over?" she asked.

"Gladmane told me that Flam thinks I don't have a single good idea!" Flim answered.

"Gladmane told me Flim thinks I couldn't sell heat lamps to yaks!" Flam said.

Applejack explained they were only arguing because of Gladmane. He was afraid that together they could take over his resort.

So Flim and Flam came up with an idea to reveal Gladmane's true colours and they needed Fluttershy's help.

"This is Impossibly Rich," they told Gladmane. "She's one of the wealthiest ponies in Equestria."

The brothers said that Impossibly Rich was going to build her own resort in Las Pegasus.

Flam pretended Impossibly Rich didn't believe Gladmane could keep his resort open without his employees leaving sooner or later.

"What stops them from just leaving to join any competitor?" Flam asked. Unfortunately, Gladmane saw through their trick and realised that Impossibly Rich was in fact Fluttershy in disguise!

"Never try to con a con-pony," said Gladmane and he walked away laughing.

Later, Applejack and Fluttershy confronted him in his office. Fluttershy told him it was mean to keep ponies from getting along for his benefit. But Gladmane didn't care as long as it worked.

"As long as I keep 'em convinced that I'm their only friend, all of Las Pegasus will be mine. You can't trick a confession out of a pony like me! I'm always one step ahead," he boasted.

But Applejack revealed that the loudspeaker in Gladmane's office was on and everypony at the resort had heard the whole thing.

"Flim and Flam told us you'd see right through the fake rich pony and that once you did, you wouldn't be able to resist gloatin' about it. This was all part of the plan!" Applejack explained.

Now everypony could be friends again.

With all of the friendship problems solved, Applejack and Fluttershy's cutie marks glowed.

The Cutie Map was right to send them both to Las Pegasus after all!

the end

28 Pranks Later

Fluttershy was in the forest when she realised she had lost track of time. It was very dark and the forest was full of scary noises. She saw a pair of glowing eyes and then the outline of a huge creature emerged with a horrifying wail.

Fluttershy was terrified until she heard … laughter. It was just Rainbow Dash pulling a prank. The problem was nobody except her found it funny.

The next day, the friends met to talk to Rainbow Dash about her pranks. She thought they were harmless, but the others tried to convince Rainbow that a prank wasn't funny if she was the only one laughing.

Nothing the other ponies said could convince Rainbow she was doing anything wrong. The only thing she knew was that she had to try even harder to think of better pranks.

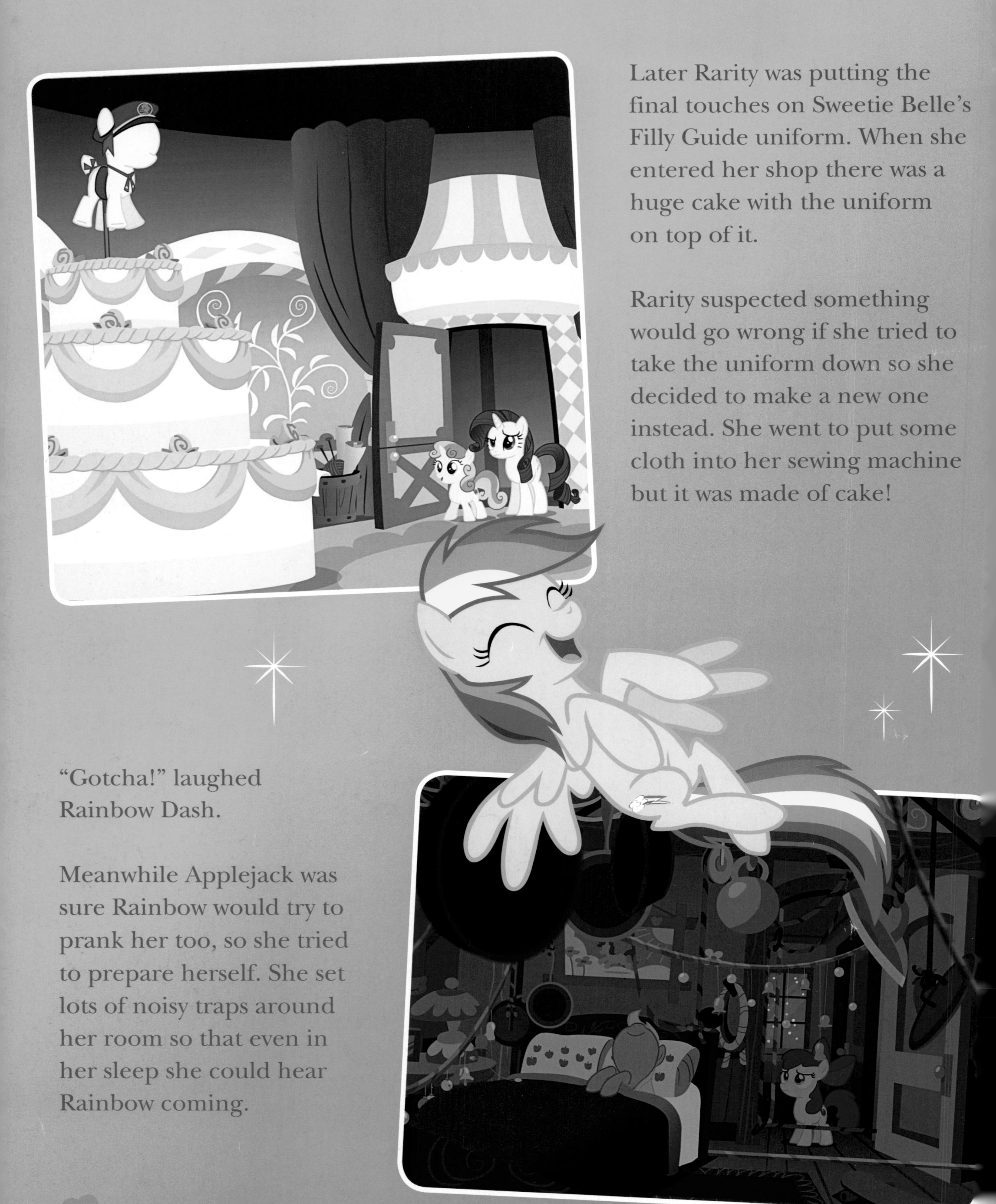

Later Rarity was putting the final touches on Sweetie Belle's Filly Guide uniform. When she entered her shop there was a huge cake with the uniform on top of it.

Rarity suspected something would go wrong if she tried to take the uniform down so she decided to make a new one instead. She went to put some cloth into her sewing machine but it was made of cake!

"Gotcha!" laughed Rainbow Dash.

Meanwhile Applejack was sure Rainbow would try to prank her too, so she tried to prepare herself. She set lots of noisy traps around her room so that even in her sleep she could hear Rainbow coming.

But when Applejack woke up the next morning, she was outside in the pig pen!

Rainbow Dash kept pranking the ponies and by the end of the day, everypony had had enough. They went to ask for Pinkie Pie's help.

"Are you honestly going to stand there and tell us you know nothing about all of Rainbow Dash's pranks?" asked Rarity.

But Pinkie Pie thought Rainbow's pranks were funny. When the ponies asked her to stop Rainbow from pranking them, Pinkie didn't know what to say.

She loved to joke but she understood that perhaps Rainbow had gone too far.

Pinkie went to talk to Rainbow Dash. But before she could say a word, Rainbow told her the idea for her biggest prank yet.

Rainbow was going to replace all the Filly Guide's cookies with her own, special ones. The prank cookies would cause ponies to have a 'rainbow mouth'. Pinkie Pie didn't think this was very funny and suggested that maybe it was time Rainbow Dash stopped pranking ponies for a while, but Rainbow wouldn't listen.

The next morning, Rainbow visited Pinkie for help with her prank.

But Pinkie wasn't feeling very well. She had a rainbow mouth and a craving for Rainbow's cookies. So Rainbow Dash left to prank alone.

Rainbow Dash was supposed to help the Cutie Mark Crusaders sell their cookies for the Filly Guides.

"I don't want none of your pranks ruinin' the night," Applejack warned her.

"I'll be with you the whole night so you can keep an eye on me," Rainbow reassured her.

A few hours later almost all the boxes of cookies were sold and it was getting dark. There was nopony in sight and the streets were eerily silent, except there were a lot of empty cookie boxes on the ground. Rainbow went to Pinkie Pie's house to see what was happening.

Inside she found Mrs Cake, Pound Cake, Pumpkin Cake and Pinkie Pie with rainbow mouths, calling for cookies and behaving like zombies!

Rainbow Dash flew out of the bakery and saw everypony in town behaving the same way. Rainbow Dash found Applejack, Rarity and the Cutie Mark Crusaders, who luckily seemed fine. She took them to a barn and boarded it up from the inside.

Rainbow Dash said it was all her fault because she had replaced the Filly Guides' cookies with joke ones. But she never meant for everypony to get sick!

Little did she know, Rarity, Applejack and the CMCs had all eaten the cookies and were beginning to turn into zombies too!

The ponies outside the barn broke in and now Rainbow was surrounded!

"Coooooooookiiiieeeees …" the Cutie Mark Crusaders moaned.

“We want cookiiiiiiiieeeeeeees …” Pinkie Pie droned.

“I never meant for this to happen, it was just a harmless prank! It was supposed to be funny but this isn’t funny at all!” cried Rainbow Dash.

“Exactly!” said Pinkie Pie in her usual cheerful voice.

Rainbow’s jaw dropped. “What? Wait … What’s happening?” she said, thoroughly confused.

“Oh we’re just pranking the prankster,” Rarity answered calmly.

When Pinkie Pie couldn’t convince Rainbow to stop joking around, she had thought of a better way to make her realise what she was doing. And the whole town had helped her!

“Pranks can be a lot of fun when everypony has a good time. I just thought you needed to see what it’s like when they don’t,” Pinkie Pie revealed.

And Rainbow Dash finally understood!

Party Pooped

Twilight Sparkle was pacing nervously. A group from Yakyakistan was visiting the Castle of Friendship and Twilight hoped to make new friends. She wanted everything to be perfect.

The yaks were also very curious about the ponies.

"Yaks hope for great friendship between ponies and yaks. Friends for a thousand moons!" Prince Rutherford said when they arrived at the castle.

Twilight invited Prince Rutherford to a banquet of traditional yak foods.

"If things not perfect, yaks get mad," Rutherford warned her. "Yaks always get mad when things not perfect!"

But the food didn't taste like real yak food so the yaks got angry and destroyed everything! Everypony was scared of the yaks, except for Pinkie Pie who still thought yaks were super cool.

Twilight Sparkle asked Pinkie Pie to show the yaks around town and make them feel welcome.

First she took the yaks to their sleeping quarters in the Apple family barn. The yaks seemed happy until they inspected the hay.

"This not yak hay!" Prince Rutherford roared. "Not perfect! Yaks destroy!"

Pinkie Pie tried to distract the yaks by inviting them to some entertainment.

"Presenting animals, Yakyakistan style!" Fluttershy said proudly. They had dressed some animals in antlers to make the yaks feel right at home.

"Animals cute," Prince Rutherford admitted. He watched the animals until one of the chicks tripped and lost its antlers.

"These antlers lie! These not Yakyakistani animals! Yaks smash!" Prince Rutherford shouted.

Pinkie and Fluttershy only just managed to save the animals. Things were looking bad, but Pinkie still had some ideas. She took the yaks to Rarity's boutique where she showed them some rare materials from the Crystal Empire. But the yaks started chewing the expensive cloth!

"This no taste like yak fabric! Yaks destroy!" Prince Rutherford bellowed.

Pinkie Pie was very upset, but Twilight Sparkle still hoped things could be mended.

"Pinkie Pie, tonight's Yakyakistan themed party is more important than ever! You'll make them forget all about this afternoon, right?" Twilight looked pleadingly at Pinkie.

"Definitely! I think. Maybe …?" Pinkie wasn't so sure of herself anymore.

Pinkie had planned an amazing party for the yaks, but now she was sure they would hate it. What could she do? There was nothing in Equestria that was exactly like in Yakyakistan, nothing would be perfect for the demanding yaks. Unless she could go to their home and bring something back!

Pinkie jumped on the train to Yakyakistan, but her journey was stopped short. Some sheep had decided to sit on the tracks so the train couldn't go any further.

Luckily, Pinkie bumped into Cherry Jubilee. She was making a delivery to the Crystal Empire which would take Pinkie very close to Yakyakistan!

The only problem was that Cherry and her ponies had been counting cherries all night and were very tired. So much so that they fell asleep pulling the carriage!

Pinkie could see they were heading straight for a ravine. She woke the ponies just in time, but the rock beneath them crumbled and the carriage fell in!

Meanwhile Twilight asked Spike to entertain the yaks with some music. It seemed everything was finally going well until the yaks realised Spike wasn't playing the piano, it was automatic.

Prince Rutherford smashed the piano and demanded to be taken to the party at once. When Twilight told him the party wasn't ready yet, the yaks threatened to return home and declare war on Equestria!

But without Pinkie Pie there would be no party and she still wasn't back from her trip!

While the other ponies were searching for Pinkie, they discovered a secret party-planning room in her house. They were amazed at how much effort she put into her parties.

Luckily, Pinkie had been rescued by the Wonderbolts, who helped her get on with her journey. She finally reached the edge of Yakyakistan. It was a difficult road and nopony had ever returned from the climb. But Pinkie was determined to succeed.

Pinkie wandered through the snow until she accidentally tripped and landed on a small yak's sledge. Pinkie was so close!

Unfortunately the little yak jumped off and the sledge started sliding backwards so quickly that within minutes she was back in Equestria!

Sadly, Pinkie went back to her party-planning room. The other ponies were waiting for her and couldn't believe what she was willing to do to ensure the party was perfect.